Darcy's Obsession

Abbey North

Published by Abbey North JAFF Books, 2022.

This is a work of fiction. Similarities to real people, places, or events are entirely coincidental.

DARCY'S OBSESSION

First edition. July 17, 2022.

Copyright © 2022 Abbey North.

ISBN: 979-8201752422

Written by Abbey North.

Blurb

A burning obsession, a rejected proposal, and a desperate Darcy. After Lizzy rejects Darcy's proposal at Hunsford, he can't accept it. He's lost everyone in the world who matters to him, and he can't allow Lizzy to slip away too. In desperation, he kidnaps her with the intent of taking her to Gretna Green before an extended stay at the familial castle. Lizzy refuses his offer of marriage again, leaving him to enact a more desperate plan.

Locked in the Scottish castle with Darcy, a man driven by demons and possessed by melancholia, Lizzy fights to deny the pull he exerts and her own passionate nature. Darcy sets about unlocking her inhibitions, but can she ever risk letting him win her heart?

While Abbey sometimes writes sweet JAFF, this is strictly SENSUAL. Please be advised it has a darker tone than Abbey's other works.

Chapter One

Lizzy was still fuming as she stomped across Rosings Park, heading away from the rectory at Hunsford. How dare he? Was there ever a ruder and more insufferable oaf of a man? She was trembling in her rage at his proposal. She couldn't stand Fitzwilliam Darcy, and she couldn't imagine a man she would less want to marry. That he had the audacity to propose to her, and in such an impertinent fashion, could barely be born.

The insult of it all. Did he think she had no integrity? How could she bring herself to accept such a tepid proposal as his? She wasn't nearly accomplished enough for him, her family was a burden, and she lacked the social connections he required in a wife, but he was willing to overlook her deficiencies due to his reluctant love.

"The very nerve." She uttered the words aloud as she stopped at the top of the hill, barely resisting the urge to shout in her anger. Even the normally breathtaking view couldn't distract her from her irritation at the moment.

She continued pacing and walking for a while, nearly blinded to her surroundings. Just wait until Charlotte returned. She was sure to have a blistering mouthful to say about Darcy's arrogance. Lizzy was looking forward to sharing that with her friend, wanting someone to appreciate just how outrageous his horrible proposition had been.

She shook her head as she finally dropped to the ground, the lush grass keeping her bottom from colliding too hard with the earth. "Bloody awful man." She pushed back a dart of guilt at using the curse word. Sometimes, a situation warranted the vulgarest of terms to describe it.

She focused on slowing her breathing and heartrate by closing her eyes and relaxing. The rage she carried couldn't be good for her constitution, and she hated to allow Darcy to leave her feeling wretched. He did not deserve any space in her brain.

She shook her head, uncomprehending how she had started to soften toward him. In the three weeks he had been at Rosings Park, he'd become almost tolerable. She'd lowered her guard slightly, thinking perhaps she might've misjudged him.

Of course, she hadn't overlooked his melancholia and wondered if it might have contributed to the offending tone of his condescending proposal. The darkness about him was something she'd noticed from nearly their first meeting at the Assembly ball, because it hung over him like a shroud.

She felt for him, having been concerned about his dour moods. She'd allowed herself to consider the possibility he might need a sympathetic ear, and they might become friends. Never more than that, of course. She knew her limits, and a man like Darcy would far exceed them.

That's what she got for dropping her defenses. Somehow, he had interpreted her basic overtures of friendship and concern as something far more than they were. She supposed she should have seen this coming after the incident three days ago, but it had not occurred to her that his actions had been prompted by anything more than grief and drink.

Lizzy laid back on the grass, sighing as she tried to regain full control of her emotions. She stared up at the sky, though she was in no mood to look for creatures in the clouds. Instead, her thoughts returned to the memorial for Colonel Richard Fitzwilliam three days before.

Lizzy had never met the man, but Mr. Collins had spoken highly of him, and he hadn't been the only one. Even Lady Catherine, who was often a bitter harridan, had spoken fondly and frequently of her nephew. Darcy had clearly shared a high opinion of Richard, mentioning in passing that he was his best friend.

When the news came little more than a week ago that the colonel had been killed in battle, an air of mourning had hung over Rosings Park. Everyone had donned black, including Lizzy, though she hadn't known the poor unfortunate. She'd done her best to help where she could, mainly in lending an ear to anyone who wanted to talk about their grief and sadness.

She'd noticed Darcy had shut down, not seeking out anyone, so she'd decided to take matters into her own hands and approach him. Just hours after the service that had been organized on short notice, she had approached Darcy in the sitting room.

He'd not bothered to light any of the lamps. All illumination had come from the fireplace, casting his features in gloomy shadows that had left her uneasy. She'd noticed the half-empty decanter of some liquid beside him, and it was clear he'd been deep in his cups.

Lizzy had taken the crystal glass from his hand, wanting only to offer heartfelt sympathy and to listen should he wish to talk. Before she got out a word, he took her into his arms, settling her firmly on his lap. Realizing he was drunk, Lizzy had been understanding, though she'd still struggled to escape. When his arms locked fiercely around her, she'd had a moment of fear. The fear had melted away when Darcy buried his face against her shoulder, sobbing like a lost little boy.

Lizzy had held him until his tears quieted, rubbing his shoulder in a soothing fashion and trying not to think about how improper it was to be seated on him. He was grieving and clearly out of his mind, not thinking about decorum or anything else.

It was only when he started to kiss her that she had realized there was more to it than grieving. His lips began by teasing her neck, and she'd shivered at the sensation. It had nearly been her undoing, and if circumstances had been different, with perhaps a man more pleasant than Darcy, maybe she would've surrendered to her baser urges.

Instead, Lizzy had pushed away from him and scrambled off his lap. Darcy had seemed somewhat incoherent, and she'd chalked it all up to grief and lowered inhibitions from the amount of alcohol he'd imbibed. She had taken herself from the room immediately, pausing only long enough to alert one of Lady Catherine's manservants to check on Mr. Darcy before rushing back to the rectory.

Charlotte and Mr. Collins had either already been in bed or were still tending to Lady Catherine, but she hadn't run into them. Lizzy had locked herself in the room she was using, shaken by the encounter, but dismissing it as nothing more than the circumstances that had led to Darcy's lapse in behavior.

When she'd seen him again the next day, he seemed to have no memory of the incident, and Lizzy still wasn't certain he recalled his actions. Today's awkward, insulting proposal left her wondering if perhaps he remembered at least some of it, but she couldn't be confident it had done anything to persuade him to make the offer.

Perhaps he'd been trying to act honorably, thinking he had damaged her reputation, but she was inclined to think he remembered little if anything of his behavior that evening. This proposal had seemed to come from nowhere, though he had clearly been speaking to her on a heartfelt level.

It was unfortunate he'd been so honest with how he tried to fight his love for her, and how unsuitable he found her. Lizzy could not imagine she ever would've entertained a proposal from him in any serious fashion anyway, but one presented in such a boorish way? What woman with any self-respect would have accepted? Even had she been madly in love with Darcy, pride would have forced her to rebuff him.

Of course, she had no feelings of the sort for him. A softening of her disposition toward him did not mean she had fallen in love with him. He could be attractive and witty, but there was that ever-present cloud of doom that seemed to surround him. She had heard from Jane, delivered via Mr. Bingley, that he had been in such a state since last year, when his young sister died unexpectedly.

She was sympathetic toward him, and she even had some empathy for how he must be feeling, but she couldn't allow that to sway her into accepting a proposal that would make them both miserable. Darcy was grieving and looking for any source of comfort, so he was confused.

Even if she had been inclined to marry him, she couldn't do so in good conscience. He would surely come to his senses and regret the situation at some point, and that would make for a miserable marriage. Since Lizzy had no high esteem for the institution anyway, she would have to be seriously in love with a man before agreeing to become his wife. Knowing that ambiguity would hang over them, waiting for him to realize his folly, ensured the offer held no appeal.

For the first time in a few days, Lizzy managed a small smile as she imagined how outraged her mother would be if she knew she had declined Darcy's proposal. Fanny would likely be on the verge of disinheriting her if she realized Lizzy had refused to improve the fortunes of all the family at the expense of her own heart.

With a sigh, Lizzy closed her eyes, struggling to find a state of calm. It took some determination and concentration, but she was finally able to clear her mind. With the sun beating down on her, warming her skin and making her sleepy, Darcy's appalling proposal suddenly seemed funnier more than anything, and she giggled as she allowed herself to slumber, enjoying the afternoon nap in the fresh air and sunlight, far away from the concerns waiting at Husnford or Rosings Park.

LIZZY WOKE ABRUPTLY, startled to see it was nearly dark. She must have slept for several hours, and her body felt stiff as she sat up with a groan. Sleeping on the grass, lush as it was, was no substitute for a real bed. She let out a squeal of horror when she felt something crawling on her arm.

With a scowl, she flicked away the ant and got to her feet, quickly brushing off her body and dress before unpinning her hair to ensure she had no unwanted insect visitors accompanying her as she made the trek back.

Since it was dark, and she was hardly likely to run into anyone, Lizzy didn't bother to try to pin up her hair again. It was a difficult task without a lady's maid when seated in front of a mirror, so she could well imagine how awkward it would be if she tried in the darkness with no assistance.

She hoped she hadn't caused a stir at Hunsford, believing she might've avoided doing so because Mr. Collins was so wrapped up in comforting Lady Catherine's grief at the moment. Charlotte would likely notice her missing, of course, but if Mr. Collins were at Rosings Park, her poor dear friend was likely dragged along to accompany him.

Lizzy hurried back, finding it easy enough to make her way thanks to good illumination from the moon. It wasn't quite full, but would be within a few nights, so it lit her path, and the park was well maintained by Lady Catherine's landscapers.

She noticed the lights were on inside as she neared the rectory, and she stifled a sigh. If the lights were lit, that could mean Charlotte and Mr. Collins were home or could've simply been a courtesy from one of the servants so they didn't come home to an unlit house.

She braced herself for a blistering lecture from Mr. Collins, reminding herself that as his guest, she would have to endure whatever he chose to say. Knowing him, it would be a verbose and enduring dressing-down.

Lizzy was almost to the gate of the rectory when arms reached out from the darkness, wrapping around her and holding her against a solid body. She opened her mouth to scream, but before she could, a cloth handkerchief of fine quality covered her face. Lizzy breathed in without thought in her panic, inhaling the medicinal scent of some vapor that left her head floating and brought the world crashing down around her. Color swirled to gray before fading to black as she slumped forward, no longer able to support her own weight.

Chapter Two

Lizzy woke sometime later, feeling stiff but in a different way from she had after waking from her impromptu nap on the ground. She quickly realized her shoulders were stretched up, and her arms were bound above her head. Her legs were free, and she kicked out, trying to discern where she was. She could see little in the dimly lit room, brightened only by a fire in the fireplace. There was a cloth in her mouth that kept her from calling out, but she moaned around it.

A solid form coalesced from the shadows, and her heart dropped into her stomach as Fitzwilliam Darcy approached the bed. She recognized him even in the murky firelight, though his dark expression was more brooding than she'd become accustomed to during the last few weeks of their interactions at Rosings Park, at least until news of the colonel's death reached them.

She was afraid, but mostly, she was just angry. She tugged insistently at the rope around her wrists, surprised to find he'd taken time to wrap her skin with cloth before binding her. It offered some protection against the rope, though not enough to completely keep it from chafing her skin as she struggled.

"Easy." He spoke to her as though she were a spooked stallion as he put a hand on her stomach before sitting on the bed beside her. "You do not wish to mark your skin, Lizzy."

She glared at him, saying something completely uncomplimentary that he clearly understood the gist of, though he couldn't get the pronunciation due to the gag filling her mouth. He flinched, running a hand through his hair.

She realized the carefully arranged curls were tousled and in disarray, as though he'd repeated the motion often. As she examined him, she noted his cravat was crooked, and he'd shed his jacket. One of the buttons of his shirt was undone, and the starched insert for his collar was missing as well. She'd never seen him in such a state of dishabille, and mild concern tempered her fear for a moment.

"Please do not panic." As he spoke, he caressed her stomach.

Lizzy hated to admit that she felt sparks of heat emanating from where his palm touched her through the fabric of her dress. She shivered as his fingers traced her rib cage, hating that her body could respond in such a fashion when he was clearly the one who had abducted her.

The reminder started her attempts to free herself again. She continued to struggle with the binding.

Darcy grasped her face in his hands, holding her chin in a punishing fashion. "Stop trying to hurt yourself."

She laughed at him through the gag, but she could not find a way to communicate other than glaring at him. Once more, she frantically twisted her wrists, trying to fight the bindings holding her to the rickety bed frame.

"You must cease before you work yourself into hysteria." His hand moved down her stomach, making Lizzy gasp as his fingers trailed to the junction between her thighs. She tried to pull away, but it was no use.

Mr. Darcy lifted her skirt with one hand while firmly holding her against the bed with the other. Once past that barrier, he was quick to find the slit in the crotch of her petticoat. His finger slid inside to touch her in a most daring fashion.

Lizzy nearly choked around the gag, her body stiffening in rejection even as his finger tested her depths, lightly probing the opening she'd only dared to explore a few times when she had the bed to herself instead of having to share with Jane. He bit his lip and closed his eyes, sighing with obvious pleasure as his finger dipped into her channel, pushing until he reached the barrier of her innocence.

He immediately withdrew, pulling his finger up her slit instead to the little nub that caused such pleasure when she stroked it herself. It was a rare and wicked indulgence that she always tried to resist, but she was familiar with the sensations evoked from stroking her pearl.

It had never felt so intense when she did it herself. Darcy stroked her with skilled mastery that had her hips rising from the bed to meet each touch of his finger though her mind was rebellious, struggling to cull the urge to respond even as she managed no success.

As he stroked her, she grew slippery and wet against him, a phenomenon that was new to her. She'd become damp before while touching herself, but never like this. She was practically soaked, embarrassed by the stain she must be leaving on the bed, but all practical thoughts fled her mind when he found a particular spot that made her hips jump even higher off the bed, and she moaned around the gag.

In seconds, stars burst behind her eyes as color took on a new and vivid intensity before becoming an explosion of vibrancy. Lizzy gasped around the gag, crying out with her release, though the sound was muffled.

He pulled away from her after the last convulsions in her sheath had stopped. Lizzy watched him, drained as she was from passion and release, while he brought his hand to his mouth and licked the finger that had been inside her. The sight was unexpectedly erotic, sending a new wave of pleasure through her, though it wasn't intense enough to make her orgasm again.

Only when shame crashed over her, reminding her how horribly depraved she had been to participate in his wickedness, was she was able to look away from his finger in his mouth. Tears streamed down her cheeks, and she started to sob. How could she have betrayed herself by responding with such abandon?

Darcy moved, leaning over to lie beside her on the narrow bed. Lizzy stiffened, wanting to reject his body against hers, but his hand was simply running up and down her stomach again in a soothing fashion. "You should be able to sleep now. Please do not be upset. It is normal to have such a forceful reaction to pleasure, Lizzy."

He leaned closer, pressing his lips to the cheek nearest him to kiss her before his tongue darted out to lick her teardrops. "I only want to take care of you and make you happy. You must see that."

She turned her head to glare at him, wishing she could say all the thoughts spinning through her mind but stifled by the cloth in her mouth. She hoped her gaze spoke for her, and she suspected he must have at least a hint of what she was trying to say because he cringed. It was difficult to tell by the dim firelight, but he appeared to go pale as he sat up, turning away from her.

Darcy slumped forward, his shoulders set in a dejected posture that had her feeling a pang of sympathy despite her best efforts not to. She had no reason to care after what he had done to her. With his actions, he had ruined her, though he'd likely borne no thought for that. What did he expect her to do? Was she supposed to gladly part her legs and take on the role of his paramour, reputation and good name forever ruined?

Her cheeks flushed with heat as she recalled just how wildly she'd lost herself while he was touching her. What had come over her, to react in such a fashion? There was nothing ladylike about her behavior, and she should've had the fortitude to withstand whatever he tried to do to her.

It had taken only a few skillful swipes of his finger and a few moments to break down her will and reduce her to a creature of sensation, driven only by the need for pleasure without thought of who was giving it to her, or what circumstances had brought her here. He had destroyed her previously perceived self so easily.

She was disgusted with him, but she was equally disgusted with herself. She turned her head away from him, stifling the sobs as much as possible as she cried quietly.

Though shamed, the tears that followed were somewhat cathartic. They left her mind clearer, and with a renewed determination to escape whatever Mr. Darcy had planned for her.

He returned to her side a few minutes later, sprawling out beside her. He curled himself around her, wrapping her in his arms as best he could with her restrained to the bed. Lizzy made every effort to remain unyielding, not wanting to show any hint of surrender.

Thanks to her nap that afternoon, followed by whatever he'd used to drug her, she found sleep unattainable. He was soon asleep behind her, and she allowed herself to relax marginally. It was painful to keep her body stiff, but it was painful in a different fashion to allow herself to relax against him. It was a small sign of submission, but she had no intention of submitting. Whatever Darcy's plans for her, she would do her best to thwart them if she couldn't escape him.

SHE MUST HAVE DOZED off at some point, but she awoke early in the morning to find Darcy already dressed and waiting for her. He looked as sharp as ever, and whatever had overtaken him the night before and left him in such a sad state seemed to be managed, at least for now.

She was surprised to see a dress for her over the folding screen and further surprised when he came forward with a knife. Lizzy tensed with fright, wondering what his intentions were. Did he plan to make sure she was silent about what he had done? It seemed like he would've continued improper advances if that were his only goal. She was surprised, frightened, and confused when he brought down the knife until he used it to cut the rope binding her hands.

Lizzy immediately pulled her arms away, wincing at the painful stretching sensation as she altered her position. She lifted her hands to remove the gag, but Darcy intercepted them before she could. She tried to tug away from him, but he was too strong as he lifted her to her feet, holding her wrists at her sides. He started methodically rubbing first her shoulders and then down each arm, helping to quickly restore full circulation.

There was an incredibly intense round of pain following the numbness as it faded away, and she whimpered and cried out. When Darcy held her against him, Lizzy fought her own urge to seek comfort, somehow remaining steadfast against him as the pain slowly faded.

"I do not anticipate needing to stop at another inn, but if we do, I shall endeavor to tie you a different way this evening to avoid such pain. I have no experience with these matters, and I apologize for any injury done to you." He delivered the words in a tender voice before kissing her on the cheek.

Lizzy turned her head away from his mouth, not looking at him again until he stepped back. When she lifted a hand to bring the gag from her mouth once more, he took hold of her wrists with a warning look in his eyes.

"I am afraid that must stay in while we are around others. You can eat in the carriage, but before we set out, I have a task for you."

She shuddered, recalling how she'd come apart in his arms the night before, and utterly convinced that was what he had in mind. She was further convinced when he turned around and started unbuttoning her dress. She tried to escape him, but he grabbed her upper arms, holding her still. "Shall I tie you up again?"

She shuddered at the note of warning in his voice and frantically shook her head. After a moment of maintaining stillness, he apparently decided that would be unnecessary, and his fingers returned to dealing with the tiny buttons on the back of her dress. Lizzy had only ever been assisted by their ladies' maid at home or Aunt Gardiner's in London, so it was a foreign experience to have a man unbuttoning her. His fingers brushed against her skin, igniting the most subversive pleasure each time he touched her, though she did her best to hide any reaction of the sort.

When the dress was unbuttoned, he stripped it from her methodically. Lizzy expected him to do more, and she was unsurprised when he unfastened her corset and then pulled off her shift. She was only in a petticoat now, and she brought up her hands to cover her breasts, briefly tempted to rip out the gag and scream, but she was uncertain she'd be able to do so before he could act. If he got her restrained and gagged again, he could do anything he wanted to her. At least with her hands free, there was a slight chance she might manage to escape.

Darcy's hands were quick, yet gentle, as he stripped the petticoat from her. Lizzy was surprised when he took her hand, taking it away from her breasts, so she was able to cover herself with only one arm as he led her to the vanity near the folding screen. There was a basin of water and a cloth waiting, and Lizzy hoped he would leave her to see to her morning ablutions by herself, but clearly, he didn't trust her not to escape.

Instead, he seated her at the vanity, parting her legs in crude fashion. Lizzy tried to hold them together, but he was stronger than her. He pried them apart, though there was an almost businesslike air about him as he tended to her needs, cleaning her perhaps more thoroughly than necessary, but gently.

Lizzy was embarrassed to be sensitive and aroused by the time he had finished washing her with the cloth. She evaded her own gaze in the broken vanity mirror and looked away from him as well. She was deeply ashamed by how she was behaving with him.

After drying her and spending several moments brushing her hair, which was a sensual assault in its own right, he pulled her to her feet again. Once more, he took her back to the spot where he had undressed her, replacing her shift, petticoat, and light corset.

Instead of lifting the dress she had worn yesterday, which was soiled with grass and other stains, he lifted the fine ivory gown from the folding screen. Lizzy trembled as he pulled it over her head, lifting her arms obediently. It was of superb quality, the kind of material she had worn only once or twice in her life for very special occasions. She couldn't deny the beauty of the garment, but she feared what it represented.

For a final touch, he tied a matching bow in her hair, confining it in a loose ponytail since he clearly had no idea how to style her hair any other way. Then he slipped an ivory bonnet over her hair. It was adorned with frills and lace.

Lizzy looked at herself in the cracked mirror, and a chill went through her. She looked positively bridal, but she tried to deny the idea.

When Darcy knelt on the floor in front of her, his intention clear as he reached for a pair of new shoes to match the dress, Lizzy seized the moment. She lifted her knee and jammed it into his chin, making him cry out with pain as he reeled backward.

She didn't bother to wait to see if he fell, or if she had seriously injured him. She turned and ran, realizing as she did so that perhaps she should've waited until she had the shoes on her feet. The inn's floor was splintering in places, and she winced as her foot ran into a jagged section, slowing her attempt to reach the door.

She was within an inch of grasping the knob, lifting a hand to pull out her gag as she did so, when Darcy caught up with her, slamming her forward, though his hand protected her face from colliding with the door.

He turned her in his arms, his anger obvious. "You have proven yourself untrustworthy yet again." As he muttered the words, he reached up to tighten the gag in her mouth, tying it to the point where it was almost painful.

Still scowling, Darcy took the length of rope he had used to bind her, though it was shorter now, and once again tied her hands in front of her, this time without the cloth protecting her skin. He covered her with a cloak next and then draped a black veil over her face, which did much to obscure that she was gagged.

Lizzy tried to be stiff and resisting as he herded her from the room at the inn, pulling her down the stairs. She did her best to slow them both, but he simply lifted her into his arms halfway down the stairs, clearly growing impatient. Lizzy tried to make eye contact with the innkeeper as Darcy strode past, but she had no luck getting his attention.

"Is all well, sir?" asked the man in a gruff tone.

"My wife is feeling unwell. Would you please pack us a meal to take with us? I shall send in my driver to fetch it." Without waiting for confirmation, Darcy strode on through the inn and outside.

Lizzy struggled to take in a deep breath, noticing the chill in the air. It was considerably colder than it had been at Hunsford, and she wondered where they were. It was difficult to tell much of anything with the veil obscuring her vision, but she tentatively guessed they might be heading to the lowlands of Scotland, judging by the hills and the cooler conditions. She shivered at the thought, more from the possible isolation than from the chill, though it was definitely cold this morning even with his cloak wrapped around her.

He settled her into a carriage that clearly belonged to him. Lizzy kicked against the frame of the carriage when he placed her on the seat, hoping she could gain the driver's attention.

Darcy just laughed, though he seemed to have little true amusement. "You might as well save the effort, Lizzy. Higgins is deaf. That makes him the most discreet and reliable sort."

She scowled at him, seriously contemplating murdering him in that moment. If this was an impromptu abduction, he had certainly thought of all the details quickly. It seemed unlikely that this was an impulsive action though.

Within minutes, the driver opened the door and handed Darcy a burlap sack. Lizzy tried to get his attention, but with her hands tied in front of her, she could do little except kick her feet. The man she knew as Higgins gave her a strange look, but he didn't comment or look at her again.

Soon enough, they were underway, much to her annoyance. She sat up in the seat, abandoning the thought of kicking the door, though it briefly crossed her mind she might kick hard enough to open it and throw herself out. Only a lack of knowledge of what might happen should that occur held her back. If she ended up injured from such an attempt, she would be even more at his mercy, and she was afraid he had none.

"I shall remove your gag so you can eat." As he spoke, Darcy removed her veil before undoing the gag.

Lizzy briefly considered the idea of screaming, but it seemed pointless. She could hear only the wheels of their carriage and the thundering hooves of the horses pulling it. If Higgins were deaf, her screaming would do no good. Even if that were a lie, if he were a good enough employee, he would take his payment, do as asked, and not pose any uncomfortable questions or make speculation. She could count on no help from him.

If she weren't starving, she would refuse the bowl of porridge Darcy extended to her. She was unable to stifle a small laugh of delight when he scowled as he reached into the bag a second time, clearly grasping a handful of cereal before removing his bowl.

He shook his head. "I wonder why he chose such a method for packing?"

"Perhaps he likes to make your life difficult. I tell you now, Mr. Darcy, doing so as well shall become my new goal if you do not release me at once."

If he was moved by her threat, he didn't show it. He simply gave her an impassive glance as he lifted his own bowl and started eating from it directly, since there was clearly no silverware.

Since she had no spoon, and she was starving, Lizzy brought the bowl to her mouth and tipped it back as well, taking a mouthful of the bland porridge and chewing thoroughly. They passed the next few minutes in silence, until the food had been eaten.

When the meager meal was over, Lizzy fully expected him to try to put the gag back in her mouth, and she braced herself to fight it. Instead, he left it around her neck, and she eyed him doubtfully.

He seemed to realize what her thoughts were, and he shrugged. "What would be the point now? Higgins cannot hear you, and we seem to have the road to ourselves. You certainly have questions, and we might as well pass the time in conversation."

"We are not having a polite tea, Darcy. You have kidnapped me, and this outrage will not stand. What do you think you will gain from this? Is it your intention to ruin me, to destroy my good name and my sisters' prospects for the future with your actions? If this is a form of revenge, it is quite petty and far beneath you." She sniffed at him.

His eyes widened, and he seemed genuinely surprised. "I have no intention of ruining you, Lizzy. We shall be joined over the anvil at Gretna Green within the next few hours. Once you are my bride, no one will think twice of our elopement."

Lizzy glared at him. "I shall never marry you. Even if you drag me in front of the vicar at the anvil, I will refuse. He will not be able to legally marry us unless I agree, and I assure you, I never shall."

Darcy's expression clouded, and he was clearly angry at her words. "I had hoped you would reconsider when offered the opportunity to preserve your reputation. I wish to make you my bride, Lizzy."

"I wish for you to rot in hell, sir, but I fear we are both likely to be denied our aspirations." She grasped her hands primly on her lap as she glared at him. "I want nothing to do with you, having seen what a scoundrel you are, and you can never compel me to marry you."

He sighed, leaning back and looking resigned. "In that case, we shall forgo Gretna Green, at least for now. Perhaps you will change your mind when my babe is in your belly, and you need respectability."

She gasped at the shocking suggestion. "You have taken leave of your senses, Darcy. I shall never consent to have your child."

He seemed unconcerned by her words. "We shall see, shall we not?"

Lizzy was further outraged when he opened his valise and removed a book, clearly intent on reading and ignoring her. She spent the next few minutes hurling insults at him and demanding her release, but he remained impassive.

When she was tired of hearing herself whine, Lizzy once more subsided into silence. She stared out the window of the carriage after pushing back the drape, certain now they were in Scotland. They must be if he was planning a trip to Gretna Green. The man was insane to believe he could simply coerce her into becoming his bride.

Yet she couldn't help trembling as she considered the consequences of refusing his proposal. Already, tongues would be wagging at her disappearance, and likely many would assume she had run off with a man. Would they make the connection when they realized Darcy was also gone? No doubt, anyone who assumed she was with Darcy would likely believe she had chosen to be his paramour, since she was beneath his station for marriage. Her only hope of salvaging her reputation was to accept his proposal and last name as a form of protection.

The idea was simply intolerable. She refused to surrender her freedom and herself to Darcy's machinations. He spoke boldly of impregnating her without marriage, but she did not believe he had strayed so far from the path of propriety that he would do so. It had to be a bluff, trying to force her hand.

She almost had herself believing that until she recalled how he had touched her so intimately the night before. A man worried about decency certainly wouldn't have done such a shameful act to a woman to whom he wasn't married. Of course, if Darcy had been overly concerned about social mores, he certainly never would have proposed to her at Hunsford, let alone planned this kidnapping.

And she suspected it had been planned. Lifting her head, she cleared her throat. Perhaps it was because she was being quiet that he moved his book and looked at her.

"Do you require something, Lizzy?"

She resisted the urge to launch into a new round of demands for her freedom. Instead, she said, "It seems quite obvious you have been planning this abduction. When did you decide to take me, Mr. Darcy?"

He frowned. "I was not planning to abduct you, and I have not kidnapped you."

She snorted. "You have acquired a deaf driver and yet claim this was all spontaneous?"

Darcy arched a brow. "How extraordinary of you to believe so. I never claimed this was impromptu, Lizzy. Higgins has been in my employ for several years, and that is nothing but a coincidence."

Her eyes narrowed with disbelief. "Of course." She sniffed. "You deny kidnapping me then?"

"I do. I am simply giving you a chance to see what you declined and change your mind."

She snorted. "If that helps you sleep at night, then you must lie to yourself, Mr. Darcy. I am not here of my own volition, as you well know. But if you did not plan to kidnap me, then how was all this arranged so swiftly?"

He seemed unconcerned by her disbelief. "I arranged a marriage trip. I assumed you would accept my proposal, and I found myself unable to wait a day longer. I have lost too much of late to risk losing you as well, so after our night in the sitting room following Richard's wake, I immediately began preparations."

"You did remember." She practically screeched the words at him in accusation.

His brow furrowed. "When did I claim otherwise?"

"I...you..." She trailed off with a huff.

He eventually continued speaking. "You will find a fine trousseau waiting for you at the castle. I was lucky enough to liberate one of your garments from a laundress at the rectory to give to the team of seamstresses I had working day and night to create you a suitable wardrobe. They also created your wedding dress, though I suppose it is nothing more than a travel garment now." He sighed with regret. "Do take care of it, because I envision seeing my lovely bride wearing it." His gaze dropped to her abdomen. "Of course, it might need some tailoring should you remain stubborn long enough."

She shivered at the threat. Then she shivered again, realizing it felt more like a promise than a threat. Whatever had led to his delusions, Darcy clung to them, passionately believing he could change her mind through the threat of scandal and coercion. She was equally determined he would not.

Conversation lapsed again, though Lizzy noted with some interest later that Gretna Green was approaching. She tensed in anticipation, once more hopeful she could find a way to escape.

Alas, it was not to be. When Darcy saw the sign, he pounded on the wall behind him. She frowned. "I thought he could not hear?"

"He cannot, but he can feel the vibrations from this side."

The carriage drew to a halt a moment later, and Higgins appeared shortly thereafter, opening the door.

Lizzy started to make a break for it, but Darcy reached out and pulled her across the seat onto his lap. He looked at Higgins, clearly unconcerned by the man's opinion of him holding Lizzy in such a debauched fashion. "There has been a change of plans, Higgins." He spoke clearly, moving his lips carefully, so Lizzy assumed that meant the driver had the ability to see what he was saying since he couldn't hear it.

With a nod, Higgins tilted his head, and there was a clear look of inquiry on his face.

"We shall not be stopping at Gretna Green today, though I suspect we shall need to stop soon tend to our needs a short time after. Somewhere isolated please."

With those words, Higgins nodded, touched his hat, and closed the door. A moment later, the carriage was off again, and Lizzy wondered if she had been too hasty in refusing his proposal. She should've pretended to accept it and waited until they were in Gretna Green before imploring for help from the townspeople there. Surely, one of them would have stood up and done the right thing, helping liberate her from the madman who'd kidnapped her.

23

Chapter Three

They stopped sometime later to eat and see to their needs. Darcy insisted on escorting her to a nearby field, though he turned his back and allowed her a slight measure of trust that she would have quickly abused if she hadn't needed to relieve herself so badly.

Lizzy was surprised when they returned to the carriage to find him offering a piece of foolscap, a quill, and a well of ink. She stared at him with uncomprehending eyes. "What am I to do with that?" She lifted her bound hands for emphasis.

"You are to send a letter to your mother informing her that you have taken the opportunity to act as a travel companion to my dear sister, Georgiana."

She frowned in confusion. "I have heard Miss Georgiana is dead?"

Darcy flinched. "Yes, but I doubt your mother knows that. I am trying to diminish your family's worry about you. If you prefer your mother remain ignorant about your whereabouts, that is your choice."

Lizzy, of course, did not prefer that. "Unbind my hands."

He hesitated for a moment before gesturing for her to lift her arms. When Lizzy saw the knife appear from his boot, she trembled anew, though she was certain he was only going to use it to cut the rope. He did so a moment later, and she reached for the quill, dipping it into the ink before writing her mother a letter.

Lizzy contemplated what to say for a moment, hoping she could find a way to be clever and indicate to her mother she was in distress but feared any attempt would be useless. Fanny wasn't one to pick up on subtleties, and Lizzy often felt like her mother didn't know her that well.

It seemed unlikely she would recognize anything out of character that Lizzy might include in the letter.

"You will dictate exactly as I instruct." Darcy glared at her. "I will ensure that is what you have written and nothing more."

Lizzy scowled at him, once more tempted to refuse to comply. If she wrote this letter to her mother, no one would be looking for her. She would be consigning herself to escaping only on her own means and opportunity. Yet it seemed unbearably cruel to allow her mother to think she had run off foolishly or was risking her reputation.

She could well imagine Fanny taking to her bed and wailing for days on end. Even worse, she was certain her father would be truly aggrieved, and his mourning would be deeper than Fanny's by far. He would likely closet himself in the isolation of his library, though she doubted he would do much reading. He would brood and worry, and that seemed an unforgivable sin against the man whom she loved so dearly.

With a terse nod, she said, "I am ready." Faithfully, she dictated exactly what Darcy told her to write, somewhat disgruntled to realize he phrased it in a way that sounded natural to her, so she could have written it herself. Did he somehow know her that well? She discarded the notion. He might think he knew her, but if he truly did, he would know she would not surrender even with the cruelest villainy he might plan.

When it was finished, she handed the paper to him along with the quill and ink. He sealed the ink and returned it to his valise before reading what she had written. With a nod to indicate his satisfaction, he removed a stick of wax and the Darcy seal, along with a match kit, from his bag.

She watched impassively as he opened the kit and removed the flint and striker to create a spark. The sharp scent of sulfur followed, and she wrinkled her nose as he used it to light a stubby candle kept in the kit. She couldn't help admiring how easy he made it all seem, especially in a moving carriage, before holding the wax to the flame. Then he pressed it to the paper and used the crest to seal the letter.

It was likely he normally carried the match kit with him, but if not, he'd clearly thought of everything. She allowed a small smirk as she wondered how he planned to see it delivered if they were going to be isolated somewhere in Scotland.

He blew out the candle and packed away everything except the letter before addressing her again. "Thank you, Lizzy. I am certain this will bring much comfort to your parents."

She glared. "Do not pretend to care about my family."

Darcy frowned. "I do care, at least because I care about you. I know how much they mean to you, though you consider your mother somewhat a burden. I do not wish them to be upset by our long honeymoon. It is better for them not to know the details as we work out these problems between us, do you not agree?"

She crossed her arms over her chest. "I do not think you genuinely care about my opinion on anything, Darcy, or I would not be here. I firmly and soundly rejected your awful proposal, and a true gentleman would have accepted that gracefully."

His expression darkened. "Perhaps I was a gentleman once upon a time, but that is a luxury for one who has never experienced loss or learns how quickly it can come upon you. I cannot bear to lose you too, Lizzy. Once you have accepted that and realize the depth of my affection, I have no doubt you will find reservoirs of your own."

She shook her head. "You are truly delusional. Perhaps you should return to England. I hear they have an excellent facility at Bedlam."

He scowled. "Believe what you wish, but I am not crazy. I am completely in my right mind."

She shivered a little. "The idea that you could plot something so dastardly while of sound mind truly frightens me, Darcy."

Chapter Four

Other than one more aborted attempt to escape when Higgins stopped early in the evening to allow them to see to their needs, which Darcy quickly thwarted before deciding to tie her up again, binding her wrist to his this time, they arrived at their destination without incident. Lizzy was impressed in spite of herself, eyeing the forbidding castle. "How did you come to be in possession of this?"

"I inherited it from the Matlock side of my family, Lizzy." As he spoke, Higgins opened the door, and Darcy stepped out, taking her along with him.

She looked at Higgins, seeing his eyes widen with shock as he caught a glimpse of their hands bound together. She mouthed, *"Help me,"* with great precision. His eyes widened further, indicating he'd understood, but he quickly looked away.

With a sigh of irritation, she assumed she would find no help from him. Perhaps there were other servants who could assist her. Not everyone would turn a blind eye to her situation. Even though Darcy was rich and powerful, there must be people who would be unwilling to compromise all decency and good morals to allow the charade to continue.

"See that our trunks are delivered upstairs, and you can bed down for the night. Head back to London in the morning, Higgins. I shall not need you to return for at least a month."

She gasped in shock, digging in her heels as Darcy started pulling her into the castle. She could not be stranded here for a month.

Darcy paused, reaching into his jacket. "Be sure to post this for me when you have returned to civilization." He held out the letter she had written her mother, and Lizzy's heart dropped when the servant took it with a nod and tucked it into his own pocket. She sent him a look of reproof, but Higgins was clearly avoiding her gaze. Perhaps he felt some guilt about what he was doing but certainly not enough to interfere.

When Lizzy continued to resist, Darcy took out the knife. She was no longer quite as afraid, so she stood stoically while he used it to sever the binding between them. Before she could even think about acting, he moved forward and lifted her, slinging her over his shoulder so that her head was roughly parallel with his buttocks, her loosely confined hair falling almost to the ground. He held her tightly against him, his hand firmly on her buttocks, as he climbed a long set of stone stairs once they were out of the courtyard and in the keep.

He seemed to know exactly where he was going, and though the interior was dim and dusty, he soon had an oil lamp lit, using one hand to do so. She was reluctantly impressed by his dexterity, though she didn't fight him for the moment. She didn't want to risk having an oil fire start and kill them both. "I can walk," she said grudgingly.

He hesitated for a moment before lowering her to her feet. He grabbed one of her hands with his, holding her firmly as he marched her beside him up several flights of stone stairs.

Lizzy briefly admired the castle, finding the requisite tapestries on the walls. Some were threadbare and clearly frayed, so she had no doubt they were authentic to the age of the castle. Others appeared to be more modern, but mostly faithful, renditions.

He led her up yet another flight before finally opening a set of wooden doors. He pushed her inside gently prior to following suit. When he indicated she should take a chair by the fireplace, Lizzy did so reluctantly. Darcy started to kneel to start a fire, and her gaze went to the implements beside the fireplace. The cast-iron poker would surely do serious damage to his skull, and her hand clenched as she contemplated reaching for it.

He must have grasped her intentions, because he stood up abruptly. "A fire can wait." He started pacing, always between her and the door. She watched him awhile before she grew bored with his incessant activity and looked around the room instead. It was old and dusty from disuse, but there was a massive fourposter bed with natty-looking curtains. She grimaced. "I do hope you thought to include fresh linens."

"Of course. We only have to wait for Higgins–" Before he could finish the thought, there was a knock at the door.

Lizzy braced herself, considering running, but Higgins was blocking the door as he brought in several trunks, clearly having taken time to carry up all before bringing them into the room. When he had finished twenty minutes later, Darcy slipped him a paper banknote, whispered something to him, and closed the door, locking it behind Higgins.

He turned to her. "I do hate to impose upon you, but if you wish for fresh linens, I suggest you change the bedding. I will see about finding us some food."

She scowled. "You must have servants for that?" She was not above such tasks, but she was hoping to see one of his servants and elicit help—preferably before the sole conveyance returned to England.

He shrugged. "I may consider engaging someone locally after a time, but for now, it shall be just the two of us once Higgins returns to London."

Lizzy was stymied and annoyed at the lack of options. She'd pinned her hopes on finding a sympathetic servant who might pass along a note to get her out of the situation even if they would not take an active role in helping her escape otherwise.

Disgruntled, she watched him walk to the door. He had a key that was fastened to his waistcoat by a fob, similar to his pocket watch. Clearly, he planned to keep it on his person at all times. He opened the door and passed through, and the lock clicked seconds later. Once she heard his footsteps moving away, she got up from the chair and quickly rushed to the door, trying the knob. It would turn, but the door was solidly latched into the frame. The lock was thick and impenetrable, at least in the amount of time she had.

Lizzy paced, considering her options. She hurried over to the window, pulling aside the thick drapes to find an un-paned opening in the bricks, but it was a death trap. She could likely fit through it, but there was no balcony outside, and it was a steep drop down the wall of the castle. Likely, it had been built that way to deter anyone from climbing up, and it certainly prevented her from climbing down unless she had a long length of rope.

She returned to the room, eyeing the bed linens. She started stripping them, but not with intention of changing them. Instead, she tested the strength of the old linens, disappointed when the velvet bedding started to shred with only the slightest amount of pressure.

Perhaps if she tied them together with the drapes, she might have an adequate length of fabric to escape, but it would be structurally unsound, and the fabric could rip at any moment. She was anxious to escape Darcy and what he wanted from her, but not so eager that she was yet willing to risk her life to do so.

With nothing else to do, she decided to finish stripping and change the linens. Sorting through the trunks, she quickly found the bedding and towels. She also came across the trunk that was clearly meant to be her trousseau. There were fine, exquisite items inside, of such a sensual nature that she was blushing fiercely just looking at them. The trunk included only two dresses, and she had the chilling thought that perhaps he didn't plan to let her wear much more than frilly underthings.

Setting aside the thought while resolving to resist, she replaced the bedding, finishing shortly before she heard the lock click. She contemplated rushing forward to try to catch him by surprise, but since the door opened by pushing into the room, she would have little advantage or the opportunity to hit him as she would have if it pushed outward. He would be in before she could get past him.

Instead, she hovered near the bed, stomach growling to her annoyance when he produced a tray of crusty bread, three types of cheese, and a jug of red wine with wooden glasses. Some of the tableware looked authentic as well, and she was surprised at how well it had held up. She approached, eyeing the wooden spoon and bowl thoughtfully. "Are these from the same period as the castle?"

Darcy chuckled. "No, not at all. For a time, my mother occupied herself with redesigning and redecorating the castle, intent on restoring every touch of authenticity. She soon discovered she disliked the winters here, and my father was complaining about the expense, so she abandoned her endeavors. You shall find parts of the castle restored to decent quality, including the chamber we're in, though she had not gotten around to replacing the bed linens. Other parts are still dilapidated from years of neglect. Perhaps if you enjoy living here, we shall see about restoring it."

Lizzy glared at him. "It matters not where you choose to live, Mr. Darcy. I could never be happy under any circumstances if I am forced to cohabit with you."

He looked away, blinking. His expression revealed a hint of pain, and Lizzy hated that she felt pity for him and a dart of guilt for her words. She couldn't let her own sympathetic nature sway her into accepting his behavior or endorsing anything he had done. To do so risked normalizing it and only encouraged him to believe he could win her over eventually.

Once the food was gone, Lizzy couldn't stifle a yawn. She was tired, but she dreaded that he would truly follow through on what he'd threatened. She eyed the bed doubtfully, seated at the table in the hardback chair still. "Where will you be sleeping, Mr. Darcy?"

"In here." He seemed startled by the question.

She glared at him. "And where shall I sleep?"

"Beside me, Lizzy."

She shook her head. "I cannot do that. We are unmarried. It would be most improper."

"It is what it is. In my heart, we are already married, so I see nothing wrong with it. To get you with child is the only way to ensure you will preserve my reputation and your own, and that can hardly be accomplished without sharing the marital bed."

She glared at him. "There is nothing marital about it, and you will have to force me. Is that what you want, Darcy? Are you willing to have me under such sordid terms?"

He eyed her for a moment, his expression considering. "I do not think it will come to that. You cannot deny your own passionate nature, Lizzy. You came apart so beautifully in my arms before. I believe you will find it is yourself you have to fight far more than me."

Lizzy shuddered at the words, primarily from fear, but more from the fear that he was right than fear of him. She could not resist earlier, so what made her think she could do so when she tried this time?

Panicked, Lizzy stood up and raced for the door. Darcy blocked her, catching her in his arms and pulling her to the bed. She fought him, but she still ended up pinned underneath him. As much she hated to admit it, part of her enjoyed being in the position with his strong body securing her to the mattress, his hands holding her wrists.

When he started to kiss her, she turned her head away, and his lips coaxed teasingly along her jawline instead. He nipped her neck, and she trembled at the sensations overtaking her. She didn't want to want him, but it was useless to pretend, at least with herself, that she did not.

She might hate him, and she certainly didn't trust him. She even feared him and how unhinged he might be, of what actions he might be capable, but that didn't keep her body from responding to his overtures.

Once more, she said, "This is not what I want, Darcy." She tried to sound confident as she projected the words, but there was a hint of breathlessness in her tone she couldn't hide as he released her wrists to flick his thumbs across her nipples.

He ignored her words as his lips softly touched hers. They coaxed her to respond as he kissed her, making her gasp and her lips part. Darcy ran his tongue across her bottom lip before easing inside her mouth. She knew she should pull away, turn her head, or perhaps even bite his tongue, but the feather-soft kiss started sensations deep in her belly, and instead of turning from him, her body sagged as it relaxed into the embrace.

She brought her hands to his shoulders, telling herself she meant to push him away even as she dug her fingertips into his firm flesh. When his tongue stroked over hers, she massaged it in return before trapping it against the side of her mouth, between her cheek and teeth, sucking lightly before she nipped him.

He let out a startled grunt, and the kiss changed from sweet to passionate in the blink of an eye. The force of his kiss strengthened, and all she could do was surrender to the maelstrom of sensations. Denying her own response would be like standing in front of a herd of stampeding horses, trying to remain on her feet and pretend they weren't bearing down on her. She couldn't feign she was unmoved.

His mouth slid down to her chin and across her neck. Her stomach fluttered as he skimmed her carotid artery with his tongue. She moaned when he sucked firmly at the bend of her neck, a conflicting array of sensations accompanying the gesture. Chief among them was pleasure, but with a heavy dose of guilt for enjoying herself. When he finally lifted his head to look down at her, she let out a sigh of relief that she didn't have to keep fighting herself for the moment.

He paused then, a look of determination on his face as he spent the next few minutes disrobing her. Lizzy made it as difficult as possible, but for all her resistance, she still found herself pinned under him again moments later in almost the same position, though they were both undressed now. She shivered at the feel of a naked male body against hers. She had never seen a nude man before, let alone been so close to one. She was uncertain how to feel that it was Darcy who should be the first.

Dismay. Desire. Confusion. Anger. Need. They all blended inside her head, leaving her confused and temporarily pliant. He took advantage of the moment to inflict another drugging kiss before once again gliding his tongue down her body and repeating the nip on her neck, but with more teeth this time. In spite of herself, she moaned as the sensation sent pulses of pleasure through her cunny.

Darcy moved lower, nibbling his way toward her breasts. Each nip her flesh sent a spark shooting through her, but the closer he got to her tender nipples, the tenser she became. She held her breath and braced herself as his mouth encompassed one of her nipples, and she couldn't hide the pleasure as he started to suck firmly.

She arched her back and thrashed beneath him, uncertain if she was trying to escape the touch or deny her own willingness to proceed. When Darcy released her nipple, she almost grumbled in disappointment. Clinging to the last shreds of self-control helped her hide any response, but she was a wreck on the inside.

Lizzy was devastated by how quickly she was surrendering to him, ceding all control to the man pinning her to the bed. She wanted to be strong and defiant, but it felt so good to have him touch her, and part of her, deep down, felt like she had been waiting for such passion all her life, despite believing she had dismissed the possibility such emotions and feelings existed.

She cried out with shock when his tongue traced her breast before nibbling on the underside. Lizzy threaded her fingers through his curls, uncertain if she was going to pull him closer or push him way.

Darcy moved laterally across her chest, licking the flesh as he went. When he reached her left breast, his tongue swirled around the taut nipple before his mouth engulfed the fleshy part, sucking forcefully. She whimpered at the pleasure. "What are you doing to me, Darcy?"

He lifted a shoulder in a half-shrug. "I want to make us one, Lizzy. I want to touch and kiss you, to see your pleasure, and to leave my emission in your sweet little cunny. I am claiming you."

"What if I do not want that?" It was an ambiguous question, made even more unclear by the fact she didn't know the answer herself. In the cold light of day, she would firmly reject such a thought, but it was more difficult to be dispassionate when they were entwined so intimately.

"You certainly seem to want what I am offering you, dear Lizzy." His hands had moved down her body as his mouth went farther south, and he stopped the slow way he had been advancing downward an inch at a time.

He went straight to her cunny, which was far too easily displayed to him by her nakedness. His fingers slipped into her opening, finding her wet and easily accommodating two of his fingers. "It feels like you want this too."

She wanted to deny that, but then she would look like a fool and a liar since her juices gleamed on his fingers when he lifted his hand to his mouth to suck them clean. It reminded her of how pleasurable she had found it when he first did that at the inn. She was shamed by her reaction even as a rebellious part of her wanted to take what he offered, and damn the consequences.

What would be the harm of having an affair with Darcy? She had no intention of marrying, after all, so her virtue mattered not. If only there was no risk of bearing his child…

"Delicious." His mouth resumed its trail southward, licking her stomach as he went. She shivered at the pleasure. Despite her own inner turmoil and the circumstances that had brought her here, she couldn't deny she wanted Darcy regardless of all the reasons why she shouldn't.

She winced when he veered to the left to suck firmly on her hip. Darcy extended his tongue, and she trembled as the damp appendage moved down to her quim. Her heart was racing in her ears, and a voice in the back of her mind was demanding she stop this wicked prurience right now.

As his fingers explored her, she shook under the force of the sensations. She couldn't allow this to continue. It was terribly improper even if they had been married. She opened her mouth to demand he stop, but all that emerged was a deep and husky moan when his tongue targeted her pearl.

He lapped at her slit before tracing her nubbin with the tip of his tongue and sucking firmly. Looking down, the sight of him between her splayed thighs was erotic torture. It shouldn't feel so good to have the man who had arranged her kidnapping between her legs.

She gasped when he sucked forcefully on her clit before nibbling the inside of her mound. Her breath felt trapped in her throat when he plunged his tongue inside her puffed lips. She hovered on the edge of coming, whimpering as the pleasure built and headed toward a final explosion. At the last moment, he flicked his tongue underneath her pearl in a particularly sensitive spot that sent her into a trembling orgasm.

Her body shook under the intensity of release, and she was so lost that she didn't realize he was staring at her for a moment. When she could focus again, she met his gaze boldly, though she felt tremulous inside. "Are you finished savaging me, Mr. Darcy?"

He scowled. "Do not pretend you were unmoved by the passion between us. You enjoyed my touch and the feel of my mouth on your cunny. To pretend otherwise makes you a hypocrite."

His words were like darts of guilt piercing her with their authenticity. The truth was too humiliating to acknowledge, so she averted her gaze, holding her breath to see what he would do next.

His hands went to her hips. He clenched them tightly and shifted her so that her pelvis was angled upward. She shook her head, exhaustion and lethargy competing for supremacy inside her. "Not tonight. Please."

His expression was stern. "Tonight, and every other night. You are my fiancée and my world. I would give you everything if you will only accept it. In return, I want only your love and submission to the passion between us."

She shook her head as she drew in a ragged gasp, pleasure soaring through her as the head of his cock pressed to her opening. "I do not submit or agree to anything. You stole me from my home, sir. How can you possibly believe I will cooperate with your vulgar desires?"

He chuckled softly. "Yes, I did, but no matter how I manipulate the situation, I cannot force your body to respond. Only you control that, sweet Lizzy, and your quim is dripping for me." With those words, he drove inside her completely, surging as deeply as he could and burying his shaft to the hilt.

Lizzy cried out at the intrusion, never having expected such discomfort. "Please... It hurts."

He gritted his teeth together, looking pained but determined. "I cannot. It is best dealt with quickly, and then pleasure may resume."

She tossed her head, rejecting his words. "Impossible. This is unbearable." As she spoke, he pulled back and surged inside her again. She cried out anew, though she realized his second thrust hadn't been nearly as painful.

Tears rolled down her cheeks as he pulled out once more before easing into her more slowly. She caught her breath as pleasure started to overtake the pain, staring up at him in confusion.

His smile was tender. "Surrender, my love. I promise you will enjoy what comes."

"No." The word was meant for herself more than him, trying to reject and refuse to acknowledge her body's reaction to the man holding her captive.

She didn't want to be wet and aching with need, and she didn't want the walls of her sheath to conform to him and cling to Darcy's cock as though desperate to keep them fused. She didn't want to feel aching desire deep in her womb, and she certainly didn't want to lock her thighs around his waist, but she did so just the same.

"You look magnificent like this, so conflicted and angry, yet so wanton and aroused. If I could, I would keep you just like this all the time." He thrust in and out of her forcefully and rapidly, sending renewed sparks of arousal shooting through her.

He took her masterfully, like a maestro leading a symphony. He directed her body to perform to his specifications, and though she wanted to fight it, and was desperate to deny to herself how much she liked it, she was swept away by his touch and control.

"I am nearly overcome. Soon, I shall spill inside you, and we will be one." His base words made her spasm underneath him as another orgasm broke over her, making her cling tightly to him as she cried out her pleasure.

The first spurt of his release brought a slight return to reality when she realized there was nothing blocking him from emptying inside her. She was too immersed in pleasure to think deeply of it, but she was aware he might have made her pregnant.

In that moment, she was shocked to find only pleasure in the thought. Her reaction woke her up enough to push him away as he finished spending himself, leaving a deposit of his gism on her thigh as she rolled away.

With a grunt, he pulled her back, collapsing atop of her, his weight pressing her into the bed, but in a strangely reassuring and comforting way. She shouldn't be curled up against him like this, and she definitely shouldn't derive pleasure from having him hold her after he had just taken her like that. Her mind was unreceptive to logic or reason, so her body found no strength to move.

Eventually, he eased onto his side, taking her with him. Darcy pressed a tender kiss to her shoulder before biting the same spot more firmly. "Rest now, Lizzy. Now that you are my lover, I intend to have you on a frequent basis, so you shall need to recover."

She blinked as sleep tried to overtake her. "This is complete madness. You cannot keep me here. You cannot do whatever you want with my body. Your mouth down there..." She flushed before saying with a prim note, "That is most unnatural."

"Perhaps it defies conventions of society, but I do not care." He opened one eye, which appeared glassy from deep satiation. "Whatever we have is between us, natural or unnatural. You belong with me now, and I am going to have you until you hear *my* heartbeat every time blood pounds through *your* veins."

She shook her head, though her heart wasn't in the protest. "If you will not release me, will you at least spare me the fate of being consigned to role of plaything, subject to your every whim?"

He let out a dark laugh. "I cannot promise that. I shall endeavor to ensure you enjoy all manners of passion between us, and if you absolutely hate an experience, I will refrain. It was quite obvious this evening that you did not hate what we did. You were beautifully responsive, and I believe you were excited."

She shook her head, too exhausted to keep fighting with him right then. "Are you truly mad beyond all redemption then, Darcy?"

He lifted his head to look down at her, his expression inscrutable. "Perhaps. I can no longer say with confidence. What does it matter? Life is suffering and death, except for moments like these."

Slowly, she shook her head again. She didn't know just how unbalanced he was, but he was clearly on the edge and seemed determined to drag her over it with him. She should fear that more than she was able to right then.

"Now rest, my love. There are many delights awaiting us in the coming days as you move closer to your inevitable surrender."

His words frightened her, but they also inspired a heavy surge of desire inside her, which she knew was wrong. She shouldn't feel this push/pull for her abductor but had a difficult time pretending the time spent in his arms hadn't been amazing. It was humiliating, but she was eager to repeat the experience. The pleasure he could give her seemed more important than the fear he inspired, though she knew that could change in a moment.

Why not indulge in this experience? She could be a worldly woman, uncaring of others' opinions, and use Darcy much like a tutor in the arts of lust. Yes, it would be an ideal situation, and she need never submit to marriage. She refused to allow him to force her to accept that. As long as she maintained her resolve and focus, she had no reason to deny herself.

She had almost sold herself on the idea as she drifted off to sleep when she recalled his ultimate plan was to impregnate her to force their union. Her eyes snapped open, and she burst into sobs. She couldn't allow that. It would tie her to him for life.

Chapter Five

Lizzy had eventually subsided to sleep after sobbing for a while. He hated to see her so broken, so clearly torn up about her surrender. Yet she had done so with such breathtaking beauty. Watching her come undone at his hands had been the single most satisfying experience of his life.

He felt a twinge of conscience that it had come about this way, but she'd left him no alternative. When she had rejected him, he had seen his future crumbling before him. No doubt, she would soon return to Longbourn, or perhaps on to London to join her sister Jane there, and that would be the end of it for them.

He'd had to act while she was still in his sphere of influence. When he had already begun the preparations for a hasty marriage and long honeymoon, it had seemed a criminal enterprise to waste them. If he let her go, he gave up on everything.

After all, what other reason did he have to go on? He'd lost everyone he loved. First his mother, and then his father, and then George Wickham, in a sense. He'd been like a brother to Fitzwilliam for many years, so his betrayal, while unsurprising after Fitzwilliam had seen glimpses of his true self over the years, had still been a blow.

Of course, that loss and betrayal couldn't compare with what Wickham had done to Georgiana, costing him his dearly loved sister years later. Even now, rage filled him as he thought about Wickham's actions, and how they had spurred Georgiana's death. If he had the man in front of him, he wouldn't hesitate to dismember him with his bare hands. To have seen the wretch practicing his wiles on Lizzy had been more than he could bear. If he had not taken Lizzy, he likely would've ended up murdering Wickham.

He still hadn't ruled that out as a possibility, but in the past, Richard had been instrumental in talking him down. On more than one occasion, Darcy had plotted Wickham's death, only to have Richard point out the flaws in his plan.

He smiled briefly, recalling his cousin's gift for draining his madness by poking holes in the ideas he came up with rather than trying to appeal to his better nature. When it came to Wickham and revenge, Fitzwilliam no longer believed he had a better nature.

He turned slightly, staring at Lizzy. He put his arm around her, drawing her closer. In her sleep, she did not pull away, though he was certain she would if she had woken. She would instantly reject him. It had taken longer than he'd expected to break her resistance, but he had done so. He had to continue stoking her passion, which was the only chance he had of getting her to lose control and set aside her objections to the match.

He moved his hand lower, cupping her abdomen. There was a spark of hope in his breast as he imagined new life kindling there. The idea of Lizzy swollen with his child filled him with pleasure. It was the pure, sweet pleasure of familial bliss, with nothing tawdry about it. He longed for the moment when he could hold his wife in one arm and his son or daughter in the other.

He prayed his seed had already started to take root. He feared as stubborn as she was, she would deny her feelings until the end. Only the risk of scandal or ruin for her sisters might motivate her to change her mind. He doubted she would do so even for the sake of her own reputation, despite being one who wanted to maintain the appearance of complying with society's rules.

He suspected there was a deeper, more untamed side to her, and he intended to find it. He now knew she was unable to deny her own baser urges even if her mind wanted her to. That would be the key to unlocking Lizzy's heart.

If he failed, there was no point in going on. With nothing else left to live for, if he lost her, he would have lost everything. All his hopes for the future and any sort of happiness rested on Lizzy opening her heart to him.

If the most direct route to doing so included impregnating her with his bastard, he could live with that shame. After all, he would never allow her to remain his unmarried paramour through the birth of their child. They would have a legitimate marriage with legitimate offspring before the birth.

A baby was just an incentive to get Lizzy to see the possibilities that existed between them. He knew she did not love him yet, but if he persisted and showed her he was more than the man she believed him to be, he could get through to her. Once he won Lizzy's love, he would have everything in the world to live for, and it was that thought which kept him going.

Chapter Six

Lizzy woke to his mouth between her legs, his tongue tracing her slit before he sucked on the little nub that sent her careening over the edge into orgasm again. She was shamed by the release even as ecstasy broke over her, and she was in no frame of mind to resist or deny that she wanted him when he slid up her body, his shaft nudging inside her quim seconds later.

She was sore from last night's passion, but even as she moaned her protest, her body accepted him, molding to the length of his cock as she thrust up against him. His fingers dug into her hips, holding her against him as he plunged in as hard as he could. She was responding just as eagerly, pushing against him with all her might.

His shaft started to spasm inside her, and it triggered yet another orgasm for her. Lizzy was humiliated by how easily she came, but she couldn't deny what a rush it was, or how good it felt. He followed seconds later, spilling his seed inside her once again before holding her against him in a tender fashion.

Lizzy laid in his arms for a few moments, at first not allowing any thoughts to surface. Slowly, they started to crowd her mind as the pleasure faded until she was once again overwrought.

What had she done? She had allowed Darcy to engage her in all manners of wickedness, and she was unable to prevent her own wants and urges. He had kidnapped her, but her body had betrayed her. It didn't seem to care that he was holding her against her will. Physically, she craved his next touch as much she needed her next breath. She was disconcerted by the reaction and abruptly rolled away from him.

It was almost a surprise that he let her go. She sat up, keeping her back to him as she leaned forward. She put her face in her hands, struggling not to sob at the weaknesses her actions had revealed. What kind of woman was she to allow this iniquity? Not only to allow it, but to indulge in it?

She was deeply ashamed of herself, and it helped her jerk away from Darcy when he put his hand on her shoulder. "Do not touch me," she said stridently as she got to her feet, searching for any of her clothing from the night before. She saw her shift from the corner of her eye and turned toward it, sliding it on and still feeling utterly vulnerable, but at least her nudity was covered.

Darcy look disconcerted as he sat up. "What is wrong?"

Lizzy couldn't hold back a hysterical laugh. "What do you think is wrong, Darcy? The things you did to me..." She shook her head, closing her eyes in dismay.

He stood up and came to join her, not bothering to dress. He sounded confused, which made her eyes open as she looked up at him. "You enjoyed what we did. I ensured that."

If she could have put her hands around his neck, Lizzy fully believed she would throttle him in that moment. "It does not matter whether I physically enjoyed it. That you introduced me to such depravity, which I allowed..." She shook her head. "It cannot be borne." She was disgusted with herself, and it reflected in her tone.

"There is nothing wrong with passion. It is a gift between lovers, especially since many marriages in our social circles still take place for far more practical reasons. Take your dear friend Charlotte and the exasperating Mr. Collins. Do you truly believe there is any desire between them? Do you imagine they have this kind of passion when they are in their marital bed?"

Lizzy shuddered at the thought, and for a moment, she was briefly tempted to laugh as she imagined Mr. Collins doing one-tenth of the things Mr. Darcy had done to her the night before. She quickly banished that thought, not wanting to risk visualizing any of those acts with Charlotte or Mr. Collins's face interposed over the images currently crowding her mind. "I do not suppose they do, but—"

"Why should you not revel in the fact that we have this harmonious passion between us?"

She put her hands on her hips and glared at him. "Do not try to tell me how to feel, Darcy. Physically, I cannot deny you provoke a response, but my mind finds it abhorrent. I despise you more than any man I have ever known, and I am here against my will. If you cannot understand why I felt conflicted at finding pleasure in your arms while I hate you, then you are beyond seeing reason."

Without another word, she slipped past him, too angry to continue arguing with him. For once, her heart remained hardened to the obvious anguish her words inflicted.

TO HER SURPRISE, HE'D allowed her to dress without trying to interfere, though he had picked out the night-rail she wore, refusing to allow her to put on anything underneath it. She was self-conscious as she sat across from him at an old wooden table in the stone kitchen.

His mother had not gotten far with her renovations in this room, so there was extraordinarily little that was modern about it. Darcy had managed to toast bread over the fire and serve it along with a bowl of runny scrambled eggs that were unappealing. If she hadn't been so ravenous from the night before, she would've refused the so-called meal.

She didn't look up when he called her name, determined to ignore him. If she could pretend he wasn't there, and keep any response in check, he would soon lose interest and allow her to return home. Or so she hoped. Surely, he was wasn't so unhinged as to continue to keep her once he accepted she had no interest in him—if she could convince him.

Lizzy shuddered as she imagined the consequences of returning home. Thanks to the letter Darcy had forced her to write, her mother and father currently believed she was embarking on a respectable adventure. If she could return home soon, she could pretend she had just not gotten along well with the lady in question. Of course, she had no idea how she would explain to her parents the situation should word reach them at some point that Miss Georgiana Darcy had passed away last year.

To her horror, she nearly burst into tears as she contemplated the thought of her stomach expanding, revealing her shameful actions to all. If there was a child, she saw little alternative but to accept Darcy's proposal. How could it be otherwise? As an unmarried mother, she would be reviled by society, and not only that, but she would ruin her sisters' prospects as well.

No doubt, Mr. Bingley's interest in her sister would fade away. As it was, all they'd done was exchange a couple of letters before her sister went to London, and she knew Jane fretted Mr. Bingley was losing interest since he hadn't visited her upon or since her arrival in the city. She knew Jane hadn't seen Mr. Bingley since his abrupt withdrawal from Netherfield.

She lifted her head and glared at Darcy. "Are you the one responsible for convincing Mr. Bingley to leave Netherfield shortly after the ball, thus breaking my dear sister's heart?"

He stopped chewing and swallowed, washing down the bite with a gulp of water before he met her gaze. "I am. It is obvious Miss Jane does not return Charles's affections."

Lizzy glared at him. "How dare you presume to know my sister's heart? You know nothing about anyone."

With a frown, he crossed his arms over his chest as he leaned back in the rickety wooden chair. "It was quite obvious she did not have any particular excitement to be in his vicinity. My friend's purse is far more interesting to your sister than the man himself."

"How dare you?" Lizzy tossed down the overtoasted bread into the soggy eggs. "Jane is shy, but she loves Mr. Bingley. By separating them, you have broken her heart, and I could never forgive you for that. Even if you had not taken me and held me against my will, there would be no way I would ever accept you as my husband."

He frowned, looking upset for a moment. "I have done what I think best to protect my friend's interests."

"You have done nothing but wrong, Mr. Darcy. You are a prideful, arrogant man, and to consider yourself an expert on matters of other peoples' hearts is pure hubris." With those words, she stood up and pushed away from the table, stalking from the dining room.

She expected him to follow, and when he didn't, she impulsively rushed for the door. She tugged on the metal ring, trying to keep it open, but it was solidly locked. It took a moment to realize there was a wooden plank blocking the door, and though she might have managed to move it by herself if given enough time without interruption, she was doubtful she could do so with the threat of Darcy finding her at any moment hovering over her.

With a grunt of disgust, she turned away from the door and the great hall, finding little more on that floor besides the kitchen and larder. There was no easy way out to the back either, so she was confined to the castle until she could manage to distract Darcy in some fashion.

With a sigh of annoyance, she returned to the stairs, climbing only to the next floor instead of covering the remaining flights to the bedroom where he had taken her before. She was determined to know every inch of this castle, hoping an idea or opportunity for escape would present itself.

Lizzy ended up distracted from that goal when she entered the library. Here, Mrs. Darcy had clearly had time to work some of her renovating magic. There were old tomes, likely from the time period of the castle's construction, but they were locked behind glass for preservation. There were other, far newer volumes that had been added to the built-in stone shelves, and though they were at least twenty years old, Lizzy soon found something to entertain herself.

Taking the book, she moved to one of the velvet chaises, spending a moment dusting it off with her hand and then sneezing rapidly in succession. When the dust had cleared, she sat on the furniture, finding it more comfortable than she'd expected. It appeared to be an antique piece, though she could not venture a guess if it was as old as the castle itself. It was either a fine replica, or it had been restored.

Lizzy sat down, trying to lose her thoughts in the book, but she met with limited success. Each time she started to drift into the story, memories of the night before would flash behind her eyes. Each time, she squirmed with shame and guilt at how she'd responded with such abandon to Darcy's overtures.

If she'd managed to keep herself from reacting physically, she speculated that would've been the end of it. Darcy seemed on the edge of madness, and he was determined to claim her, but she couldn't imagine he would have forced her. If she'd maintained icy resolve in the face of his attempts to coax her to passion, he would've been stymied and left her. Instead, she had surrendered like a weak-willed chit. That would not do.

Before he approached her again, she had to find a way to build her resistance and keep herself from responding. That was the only way she could keep Darcy from taking her to bed again. Already, he might've impregnated her, stealing her choices, and she couldn't risk allowing him another opportunity to do so.

Chapter Seven

To her surprise, Darcy left her alone for most of the afternoon, not coming into the library to find her until the sun had started to set. He brought bowls of stew for them, and she was surprised to find the food passably edible after dipping in her spoon.

Darcy sat on the chaise beside her, forcing her to move her feet if she didn't want to prop them on his lap, which she certainly didn't. He lifted her book and examined it for a moment before nodding. "Excellent choice."

"Thank you." Maintaining her resolve to be cold with him, she kept her expression and her reply icy.

He flinched a little, but he didn't falter in his attempts to make conversation. Each time, Lizzy was proud of herself that she kept her replies monosyllabic and chilly.

He seemed to have indigestion by the halfway point of the meal, setting aside his stew. Lizzy was feeling similarly, her stomach a ball of nerves, but she refused to reveal that. She forced herself to eat several more bites before also setting aside her wooden bowl and reaching for her book again.

Darcy intercepted it, taking it from her hand and setting it on the table. She glared at him as she reached for it again, but he held her hands, keeping her from doing so. "Release me."

"Never," he said with clear fervor. It was obvious what he wanted as he drew her toward him.

Lizzy did her best to remain as though she were an inanimate object, keeping herself tense and frozen as his mouth settled on hers. She closed her eyes, her breath catching in her throat at the gentle way his lips explored hers.

She managed to fight her need to react even as his lips changed pressure, trying to coax her into responding. His mouth grew harder and more frantic on hers, demanding a response, and Lizzy sobbed as her lips curved to his, conceding to his demands for her passion even as she hated herself for losing the battle.

Darcy grasped a handful of her hair, tugging back her head to reveal her neck. He bit her at the bend, making her shudder with a combination of fear and pain, starkly overshadowed by pleasure at the sensation.

How could she enjoy such a thing? She couldn't deny she did when he bit her again, this time at the hollow of her throat before nibbling a line up to her chin. She gasped with shock when he bit her once more, pain making her wince even as she quivered with need.

"Say you belong to me, Lizzy." He said the words with unnerving intensity as he pulled back long enough to stare down at her, their gazes locked.

She glared up at him, finding her sense returned when he wasn't touching her. "Never. I do not belong to you and never shall, Mr. Darcy."

"Damn you, Lizzy, why must you torture me so?" There was a world of anguish in his tone, and his mouth descended on hers in a punishing fashion.

Lizzy winced at the force behind it even as a dark part of her thrilled at his domination, her mouth opening to accept his brutal kiss and return it with equal fervor. At some point, she became aware of the taste of copper in her mouth, but she couldn't be certain whether it was her blood or his.

The taste of blood helped restore some common sense, and she jerked away, turning her head from him as she struggled to reassert control. "No." She meant to utter the word in strong protest, but it came out sounding weak and unsure.

"Yes." Darcy cupped her breast through the lawn night-rail, his hand easily engulfing her through the thin fabric. Lizzy moaned when he tugged forcefully on her nipple, but she found her cunny filling with moisture at the pleasure/pain sensation. "I do not wish to be like this."

"Neither do I. I do not want to be obsessed with possessing you." His hands cupped her face then, forcing her to look at him again. "I do not want you to preoccupy every moment and every thought of my day. I do not want to feel like the continuation of my very existence hinges upon your surrender, yet here I am. You occupy my thoughts at all times, and I cannot go on without you. If I do not have you, I have nothing left. You do belong to me, Lizzy. You must admit that."

She hated to see the pain in his eyes, and the agony in his voice tore into her. Part of Lizzy wanted to confirm that she did belong to him, but the strong, stubborn part of her refused. She closed her eyes since she couldn't look away. "I do not want that. I do not want you, Mr. Darcy."

"Liar." With a sound of rage, he shoved her back, forcefully holding her against the chaise lounge. Lizzy trembled with fear even as part of her responded with delight at the animalistic side Darcy was displaying.

When he ripped open her night-rail, she didn't resist. She was still trying to maintain icy indifference even as he lowered his head, nipping forcefully on the nipple he'd just tugged moments before. That same pleasure/pain sensation shot through her, and she whimpered, curling her hands into fists in an effort to resist how she felt.

He was clearly desperate for some sort of response, and he bit her again before venturing across to suck on her other nipple. Lizzy stiffened, nearly undone by the tender rasp of his tongue against the turgid peak. His gentleness threatened to undo her far more than his angry despair, though she found it more difficult to hold out when he once again bit her, clearly driven to the edge of control.

As Darcy left a line of bites along her stomach and chest, she fought an internal battle to resist him. She could not surrender. If she did, it was tacit agreement to his kidnapping and the terms of her release. She could not give him the satisfaction.

Lizzy drew on her pride, somehow denying him the response he wanted as he spent the next several minutes trying to force or coax her to respond. He alternated between gentle and demanding, yet she managed to maintain her icy façade.

It was only when he abruptly surrendered, collapsing against her in a posture of defeat, that Lizzy had to second-guess herself. Resisting him was important for her pride, but it was obvious she was destroying him.

She owed him nothing. She certainly did not want to love him, but the broken man before her was more than she could stand. Before she could think better of it, Lizzy lifted her hand and started running her fingers through his thick curls. "Do not grieve so."

He didn't look at her. He simply turned his head away, though he didn't pull away from her. "I will return you to London in the morning. You may report me as you wish. If you choose to remain silent, I will honor that and not use these events to try to force a marriage."

That was what Lizzy wanted, but did she want it at the expense of the utter destruction of Fitzwilliam Darcy? She had no doubt he would keep his word if she continued to deny him a physical or emotional response.

She seemed to have convinced him she did not want him, and he wasn't yet so driven to desperation and madness that he would keep her if there was no hope of winning her over. She should feel a thrill of victory at having won, but all she felt was unease at her own actions, and a grim dose of disgust that she had brought such a proud man to this point.

She trembled, admitting to herself she wasn't nearly as unmoved by Darcy as she pretended. Had his offending proposal not been so insulting, she couldn't promise she would've entertained the idea of accepting, but she wouldn't have responded so forcefully and rejected him so brutally.

This moment between them was honest. Painful, ugly, and yet honest. She couldn't say she loved him, but she couldn't pretend she didn't desire him. Lizzy trembled as she relaxed against him, lifting her head so she could press a kiss against his forehead.

Darcy stiffened, turning to look at her with shock in his eyes. "Lizzy?"

With a sigh of surrender, she wrapped her arms around him, unspeaking as he shifted position so he was still covering her body while his mouth took possession of hers. She had to force herself to relax, fighting her natural urge to resist just to prove she could. How much of her relationship with Darcy was foiled by pretenses and facades they had both maintained? Could things have developed differently if they had been more open to each other from the start?

She had no time or patience to analyze the situation as his hands glided over her flesh, working her into a heated frenzy. She couldn't bear to deny or shield how she was feeling. Each caress was her undoing, every kiss or touch furthering her disassembling to rebuild as someone else. To be Darcy's lover, but more than that. She wasn't simply a reflection of the man, and there was nothing charitable about her passions. He genuinely moved her, and if it was breaking her own heart to deny him, how could she do that to either of them?

He surprised her by flipping her over, so he was lying on the chaise. She frowned down at him in confusion. "I do not understand…"

"I want to see you as you ride me, Lizzy. Take me inside your quim."

She was shy at the thought, but seeing his obvious need fueled her courage. She grasped his cock carefully, spending a moment admiring the length and surprising beauty of the male member. Having felt it inside her was different from a physical appraisal, and she was intrigued, especially at how he twitched, veins throbbing, when she slid her cupped hand up and down his length.

"Please, Lizzy." Anxiety underscored his words and sweat beaded his brow.

She couldn't bear to make him suffer anymore, so she positioned his shaft at her opening, acting on instinct and memories of the night before to ensure he was in alignment. When it felt right, she sank on him slowly, gasping as he filled her inch by inch, stretching her in a different way than he had the previous night. It was different but no less delicious or wicked, and she enjoyed every second it took to fully seat him inside her.

Darcy grasped her hips, holding her firmly as he started to thrust upward into her. Lizzy placed her hands on his chest, her nails digging into his flesh as she strove to match his pace. She soon discovered twisting her pelvis slightly added an entirely new dimension of pleasure, and she rocked against him as she pursued her release.

The climax came upon her quickly, forcing her sheath to clamp tightly around his arousal. Darcy cried out his pleasure as he stiffened inside her before convulsing as his gism filled her insides. Lizzy moaned at the onslaught, unable to verbalize how she felt in that moment.

It was only as the intensity of the orgasm started to fade that she realized she had dug her nails into his chest. She winced at the sight, though part of her gloried in leaving her mark on him. At that instant, she understood why he enjoyed leaving proof of his claim on her skin.

He urged her to lie down atop him, and she did. Darcy buried his face against her shoulder, his breathing still harsh and ragged. So was hers, and she focused on calming it. They exchanged no words, but they needed none. Their bodies had already said everything filling their minds, and Lizzy had never been more content.

Chapter Eight

That night had changed something between them. Darcy was more carefree and quicker to smile. He'd stopped asking if she would marry him, so Lizzy was wasn't forced to decide yet. She couldn't deny her passion for him, and her taciturn surrender to it was an agreement in its own right.

He'd made no further offer to return her to Longbourn, and she hadn't expected him to. She had understood what the terms her surrender entailed, though she still refused to entertain the idea of marrying Darcy or being with him permanently.

Surely this madness would pass for both of them. Yet she wondered if it ever could sometimes, especially when he was inside her, and she craved more and more of him. There were times when she strained to be one with him, making it clear desire had rapidly become hers as well.

She took satisfaction in marring his skin with her nails or teeth and was equally satisfied when he left proof of his claim on hers as well. She knew it was crazy and out of control, but it was difficult to care in the throes of passion.

As the weeks passed, her confusion grew while her emotions clouded and blended, leaving her perplexed about how she felt or what she wanted. The obvious answer was him, but her rational brain knew she shouldn't feel that way for the man who'd kidnapped her. Her emotional side no longer cared about the circumstances that had brought her to Scotland.

When she woke for the third morning in a row with a surge of nausea, she moaned as the knowledge overwhelmed her. She sat up slowly, barely managing to quell the urge to empty her stomach contents into the chamber pot as she trembled.

"You are unwell again?" There was concern in his tone but also clear delight.

Sullenly, Lizzy nodded. She could hardly be surprised that she was pregnant. There was no way to confirm it yet, but her monthly cycle was late, and now she had morning nausea and overly sensitive nipples. She had no one in her life to discuss these sorts of symptoms with, but it made sense it must be for such a reason, since she had experienced nothing like it before, and she was now engaged in a physical relationship that could lead to pregnancy.

"This is wonderful." Darcy sounded elated before his expression abruptly darkened. "No, it is not."

Lizzy's neck cracked as she turned her head sharply to look at him. "Whatever are you on about, Darcy? This has been your goal from the start."

He was pale and sweating though, looking shaken. "I did not think it through. I cannot lose you. What have I done?" With a moan, he buried his face in his hands, looking dejected.

Lizzy was completely baffled by his behavior. "I thought it was your greatest wish to see me with child so I could not refuse to marry you." She shivered as a sudden possibility occurred to her. Perhaps his obsession with her was weakening. "Have you changed your mind then, Mr. Darcy? Now that you have what you wanted, you no longer wish to keep it?"

He stiffened, obviously incensed as he lifted his head. "You shall do nothing to rid your body of my child."

Lizzy recoiled in shock. "I would never. That was not at all what I meant, Mr. Darcy. I was referring to myself. Now that you have my capitulation, perhaps you no longer wish to keep me." She tried to sound brave and disdainful, uncaring of the possibility, but her voice wobbled with uncertainty.

His expression softened, and he reached for her, pulling her into his arms. His hold was hard, allowing no escape, and Lizzy found it oddly reassuring. "Of course, I still want you. I suppose I have just realized the danger you face. I cannot bear to lose you as I did Georgiana."

Lizzy jerked in surprise. "I do not understand?" The words sounded slightly muffled with her head pressed against his chest as it was.

"George Wickham ruined my sister."

Lizzy stiffened at the claim, pulling back enough to look up at him. "I find that difficult to believe, especially since you ruined his life." She frowned. "Were his actions in retaliation for what you had done to him?"

Darcy's face turned red for a moment, and he seemed filled with rage. He trembled, but his hands were still gentle on her as he tenderly put her away from him before standing up and starting to pace. "I do not know what lies he has filled your head with, but George Wickham is the very last person you should consider any sort of victim."

"He claims you stole his inheritance because you were jealous of the relationship he had with your father." She crossed her arms over her chest. "Do you deny that?"

He paused, glaring down at her. "I bloody well do. The man presented himself falsely to my father, showing only his true self to me when we were at Oxford. I was not at all surprised when he refused the position as vicar for Pemberley upon my father's death. I wrote the man a check and sent him on his way, though that did not keep him from returning for more money. It was only on his third attempt to collect more by playing on the supposed bond between us that I denied him and saw the true extent of what a scoundrel he was. He disappeared for years after that before returning to seduce Georgiana."

Lizzy wanted to disbelieve him, but he seemed so genuinely earnest, with clear guilt and anger revealed in his expression. She shook her head. "I do not understand. Why did you not prevent such a thing?"

He flinched, the guilt in his expression growing. "I was not there. Georgiana wanted to spend the summer in Ramsgate, so I entrusted her to a highly regarded lady's companion, though now I suspect many of her references were falsified. She allowed Wickham unfettered access to Georgiana, and he seduced her."

Lizzy gasped in shock. "Not full seduction?"

He looked grim when he nodded. "He claimed he wanted to marry her. They planned to run away to elope, but I happened to show up to visit and stopped them from doing so. When I made it clear to Wickham that I would never release her dowry even if he somehow managed to find a way to get her to run away with him—it was to protect her, and not because I care a whit about the thirty thousand pounds—he soon disappeared."

Lizzy closed her eyes, able to well imagine poor Georgiana's sorrow. "What did she do?"

"She fell into a deep depression, and at first, I attributed her illness to that. I thought it was simply melancholia, especially since many in my family have suffered from it, myself included. I tried to give her space and time to heal, but when her maid came to tell me she suspected Georgiana was with child, I went to confront her. Unfortunately, the damage was done."

He trembled. "She had obtained a concoction from a woman in the village that induced a miscarriage, but it did not finish. The doctor explained later that part of the pregnancy was retained, and it made her deathly ill. She died from blood poisoning a few days later, and there was nothing to be done to stop it."

Lizzy sagged against the bed, distraught at the events he described. He was clearly heartbroken by them, and she couldn't bring herself to doubt his claims against Mr. Wickham.

She knew for a fact Wickham was the shallow sort, quite charming but with little substance. He had revealed that when he appeared to be courting her but then became engaged to Miss King.

She had insisted on maintaining the harshest view of Darcy, clinging to Wickham's assertions that he had harmed him out of jealousy and spite based on her own wish to believe rather than on any compelling conviction from Wickham's character.

Now, as the blinders fell away, she realized she had been foolish in her assumptions. There was no love lost between the two men, but she had believed the worst of Darcy because it was convenient for her to do so. She'd already thought ill of him due to his behavior at the Assembly ball and afterward, so it had seemed like more validation for her poor opinion.

She lowered her head, admitting to herself she had failed to give Fitzwilliam a fair chance to win her over. Of course, she had remained mostly unaware of his growing affection until that dismal proposal at Hunsford, but she had a moment of guilt for rejecting him so cruelly and taking pleasure in doing so.

"I am sorry I have put you in this position, dear Lizzy. I did not think it through, and if you were to die in childbirth…" He trailed off, shuddering. "I would have no reason to go on. We must return to London immediately so you can have the finest healthcare."

Lizzy sighed, torn on how she wanted to proceed. Part of her wanted to immediately accept his idea and rush back to London, but she couldn't deny part of her was happy here in the Scottish castle, though she was confined ostensibly against her will. He'd stolen the choice from her, but she had an opportunity to take it back.

She lifted her head, frowning up at him. "I do not believe there is need to rush back. I would like to become closer to you, Fitzwilliam." He flinched as she used his name for the first time, and she realized how much it must mean to him when his expression softened. "I believe it is inevitable we shall be marrying, especially in light of my pregnancy, but I wish for us to be closer first. Surely, it would not hurt to spend a few weeks here as we finish learning about ourselves and become a couple?"

He looked uncertain as he stopped pacing and leaned against the post of the bed. "I do not wish for you to be in danger."

Lizzy managed a small smile. "I do not anticipate there being any danger. I simply ask for more time. Time for you to court me without reluctant love and a wretched proposal. I need time to acclimate myself to the fate before me."

Realizing how martyrlike that sounded, she cleared her throat. "I believe I can be happy with you, and we certainly share a passionate accord. Let us spend some time getting as emotionally close as we have physically. Do you find that acceptable?"

After a hesitation, Darcy nodded. "Nothing would make me happier, but if your health is at risk—"

Lizzy stood up, approaching him so she could wrap her arms around him. "I do not believe it is. This is sincerely what I want, and I deserve the right to choose this, do I not, Fitzwilliam?"

His expression reflected his agony. "Of course you do. I have done nothing but wrong you. I have stolen choices from you, treated you with a lack of respect, and denigrated you at every turn. I fear there is little hope you can truly come to love me."

"Fortunately, I am more optimistic than you." She put her hands around his face and urged him down so she could kiss him. It was a tender, exploratory kiss that soon led to gentle lovemaking, though Fitzwilliam initially tried to resist. He clearly feared for the health of her and their child, but Lizzy was soon able to overcome his protests, and they were lost in sensual bliss.

Chapter Nine

They spent the next ten days enjoying each other, and Lizzy was starting to fall deeply for Fitzwilliam. Now that he was no longer so driven by desperation and so dark with his intentions, she could see the better side of him.

She'd seen glimpses all along, but now they were the norm rather than the exception. There were still moments when he could lose control and drive her to the brink with wicked depravities, but Lizzy was coming to enjoy and embrace those moments rather than fear them. There was a heart of darkness inside her that responded to Fitzwilliam's, making them a perfect match.

They were preparing for the return to London, having decided to make the trip back as soon as Higgins returned to check in. The driver had arrived that morning, so they were loaded and ready to depart now. Lizzy took Fitzwilliam's hand as they walked out of the castle, pausing for a moment to look around. "I should very much like to finish your mother's project of restoring the castle. It could be our summer escape."

"I shall leave it in your capable hands, Lizzy." He sighed, sounding regretful. "I do hesitate to leave. Despite some hiccups, we have found much happiness here. Or at least I have." He slanted an uncertain look at her from the corner of his eye.

Lizzy turned to look at him, making sure her expression was confident. "I have found more happiness than anything else during our sojourn. I suggest we stop in Gretna Green to make our union official before returning to England. My family will take news of our elopement far better than they will our simply running away together. I do believe it is time for you to make an honest woman of me, Fitzwilliam."

He smiled, his relief obvious. "I will be happy to do so, but I want to ensure this is your choice." He turned, putting his hands around her biceps as he looked down at her with concentration. "You truly choose to be my wife because you wish to? Or have you been forced to because of the pregnancy?" He closed his eyes, looking regretful. "That I have done such wrong..."

Lizzy pressed her fingers to his lips. "I have forgiven you for your earlier actions, and as I have told you several times now, they brought about the epiphany of my own feelings. I love you, and I choose to be with you. You cannot undo past actions, but you can accept what you have done and move forward with me. I offer myself willingly to you."

He breathed a sigh of relief before leaning down to kiss her passionately. "In that case, I happily accept everything you offer. I love you with full enthusiasm and not a hint of reluctance."

"Even though it means my mother will be part of your life?" How Lizzy managed to find the fortitude to tease him, she didn't know. She simply sought to lighten the moment, disliking when Fitzwilliam fell into the darker flashes of despair. If she had her way, she would keep him from ever reaching those depths again as they spent their lives together.

"Your mother is a small sacrifice to accept in order to have you as my wife. I believe Gretna Green is an excellent suggestion, and I shall indicate to Higgins we plan to stop this time around."

Lizzy took his hand in hers, walking with him to the carriage. She'd expected to have a slight hint of apprehension as she got inside, but she was steadfast and committed to the path she had chosen. That it was her choosing was all she required to make the choice.

She had been sincere when she told Fitzwilliam she forgave his initial transgressions against her. He had been locked in the grip of his obsession, and though that provided no excuse for his behavior, it allowed her to understand it. She was at a point where she was loving him with equal intensity, and the thought of losing him seemed unbearable. It had taken his questionable actions to allow her to face the truth of her own emotions.

She curled her hand around his, not releasing it as he sat beside her in the carriage. She looked out the window once more, a sigh of regret passing her lips. She would certainly miss their sanctuary in Scotland, but she was confident they would soon return, though she doubted Fitzwilliam would allow her to leave the range of easy and competent medical care until after their child arrived. She anticipated they could return by next summer, which made it possible to close the drapes and not tell Higgins to cancel their departure.

She snuggled against the man she would soon join in matrimony, finding pure optimism in the future. Their activities in the bedroom were just as likely to yield thorns as roses, but she was certain they would live in happy contentment together overall, and with his darkness integrating with her own, it was a match that could never be torn asunder.

He would never change his mind, and she was confident she would never change hers either. She loved Fitzwilliam and was committed to a future with him.

Epilogue

Two years later

Lizzy held little Richard in her arms as Georgie toddled across the grass in the meadow near the castle. Fitzwilliam was waiting for her, encouraging her to gain confidence in her steps. Georgiana was sixteen months, and she was just starting to run. She was a brown-eyed, brown-haired angel, and Fitzwilliam often commented how much she looked like his sister, her namesake.

Lizzy followed behind, ensuring Georgiana wouldn't fall if she missed a step as she ran, waiting until Fitzwilliam had scooped up their daughter before moving forward at a brisk pace to sit on the blanket beside them, holding Richard. He whimpered slightly in his sleep, the three-month-old disliking the disruption. Lizzy shushed him quietly, and he was soon back to the land of slumber.

She leaned against her husband, placing her cheek against his arm. "It is quite lovely here. Thank you for bringing us back in time to see the heather bloom."

"I do worry it was a bit too soon for Master Richard to travel."

Lizzy smiled. "I do not believe that will be an issue since you have endeavored to have us travel with a small army of servants and a private physician, dearest husband." She teased him about his overprotective tendencies even as she relished them.

Living with Fitzwilliam could sometimes be a bit smothering, since he was determined to keep them all safe and sound, but she appreciated that about him as well. It gave him a purpose, and as long as he had that and happiness in his life, the episodes of melancholia remained at bay.

Not that he couldn't still be a rough beast in bed sometimes, but Lizzy appreciated that about him as well. There were nights when she wanted tender love, and just as many nights, she wanted Darcy's frenzied passion that pushed her beyond her boundaries to new levels of ecstasy. They had found the perfect balance for their marriage and their life together, and she had no regrets.

"I love you, Lizzy." He said that quietly, looking at her with undeniable devotion.

Lizzy lifted her head, brushing her lips against his chin before she whispered, "I love you too, Fitzwilliam. I cannot believe how much I care, and how perfect you are for me."

"I recognize it, but I still worry sometimes that you will come to your senses. I fear I forced you into the situation."

Lizzy scowled, not liking the signs of melancholia appearing again. "Do not fear that. You know I am a most prideful woman, and stubborn as the day is long, according to my father. I would not be here if I did not wish to be." They were brave words, but they were true.

If she had not conceived Georgiana, she would've still found herself falling in love with Fitzwilliam. Now that she loved him beyond reason, she had no doubt of that. "Questioning the depth of my emotions insults me, Fitzwilliam. Do you really believe you can manipulate me to feel something I do not?"

Slowly, he smiled as he shook his head. "No, I do not. You are far too strong for such machinations."

Lizzy nodded her head sharply. "Indeed. Then do not question or insult me. Accept I know my own mind and heart, and both are decided on the matter. I have chosen you and would do so a thousand times over."

He lifted her hand to his mouth, brushing his lips against her knuckles. "In that case, I am the luckiest man alive."

"Even though my family arrives the day after tomorrow?"

He groaned. "I shall endure, and Charles will be along with your sister and their little one. I envision days spent hunting."

"And nights avoiding my mother?" she teased.

He flushed but didn't confirm or deny the suggestion. "Your mother is an interesting woman, for certain."

Before Lizzy could agree with his assessment, Georgiana reached for a pickle and brought it to her mouth. She took a bite and scowled, spitting it out with clear displeasure. It was a perfect moment, and Darcy threw back his head to laugh. Lizzy did the same, while appreciating the pure joy on his face and how it transformed him. Happiness looked good on Fitzwilliam.

PLEASE SIGN UP FOR Abbey's newsletter[1] to receive information about new releases. If you have any difficulties, email Abbey to request a manual add.

---

1. https://www.subscribepage.com/JAFF

About The Author

Abbey is a diehard Jane Austen fan and has loved Fitzwilliam since the first time she "met" him at age thirteen upon borrowing the book from the school library. He is the ideal man, though Abbey's husband is a close second. Abbey enjoys writing various steamy and sweet Jane Austen variations, but "Pride & Prejudice" (and Mr. Darcy) will always be her favorite.

Also by Abbey North

A Month To Love
Reproach (Part One)
Resentment (Part Two)
Rapport (Part Three)
A Month To Love Compilation

Crime & Courtship
Rapacity & Rancor: A Pride & Prejudice Variation
Abduction & Acrimony : A Pride & Prejudice Variation Mystery Romance
Extortion & Enmity: A Pride & Prejudice Variation Mystery Romance
Murder & Misjudgment: A Pride & Prejudice Variation Mystery Romance
Perfidy & Promises: A Pride & Prejudice Variation Mystery Romance
Crime & Courtship: A Sweet Pride & Prejudice Mystery Romance Compilation

Darcy's Courtesan
Adversity (Darcy's Courtesan, Part One)
Avidity (Darcy's Courtesan, Part Two)

Amity (Darcy's Courtesan, Part Three)
Darcy's Courtesan: A Sensual "Pride & Prejudice" Variation

Marriage & Mysteries
Honeymoon & Hemlock

Mr. Darcy's Secret Stories
Mistaken Masquerade: A Pride & Prejudice Variation
Mischief & Matchmaking: A "Pride & Prejudice" Variation

Standalone
Christmas At Pemberley: A Pride & Prejudice Variation
A Scandalous Proposition: A Pride & Prejudice Variation
Shadow of Darcy: A Sensual Pride & Prejudice Paranormal Variation
Darcy's Obsession
Blackmailing Lizzy: A "Pride & Prejudice" Variation
Darcy's Wicked Game
Danger With Darcy: A Sensual "Pride & Prejudice" Variation
Passion & Prostrations: A Sensual "Pride & Prejudice" Variation
Darcy's Debt: A Sensual Pride & Prejudice Variation
Obstinacy & Obligation: A Sweet Pride & Prejudice Variation
Heartsick: A Sweet "Pride & Prejudice" Variation
Darcy's Alibi: A Sweet "Pride & Prejudice" Variation
Never A Bride: A Fade-To-Black "Pride & Prejudice" Variation
Marooned With Darcy: A Sensual "Pride & Prejudice" Variation
Compromising Mr. Darcy: A Steamy "Pride & Prejudice" Variation
Marrying Mr. Darcy: A Sensual "Pride & Prejudice" Variation
Darcys' First Christmastide

* 9 7 9 8 2 0 1 7 5 2 4 2 2 *